HARRY POTTER

The Ultimate Quiz Book

Unofficial & Unauthorised

Jack Goldstein

First edition published in 2012

This third edition published in 2014 by
AUK Authors, an imprint of
Andrews UK Limited
www.andrewsuk.com

Contents

Introduction

The magical world of Harry Potter and his friends (and enemies!) is one that is now host to a wealth of wonderful information. Over seven books, J K Rowling has introduced us to a fantastical place where I am sure many of us would like to live – despite the risks of coming across dark wizards or scary beasts!

This quiz aims to add one more bit of fun to that world, by testing the reader's knowledge. These questions are generally based on the world as told to us in the books, rather than the series of films, as the two are sometimes quite different!

Perhaps you will try this quiz – newly updated and revised for a third edition reprint – on the bus home after a long day at work or school, or maybe you will test your friends and family to see if they are as much of a magical expert as you are. Whatever you do, I hope you enjoy answering these questions as much as I did writing them.

Good luck with the quiz!

Jack Goldstein
April 2014

HARRY POTTER

The Ultimate Quiz Book

The Questions

Harry - Part 1

1. When is Harry's birthday?

2. Where does Harry live?

3. Who brought Harry to the Dursley's as a baby?

4. What is the shape of the Scar on Harry's head?

5. What animal did Harry talk to at the zoo?

6. What was Harry's father's first name?

7. And his mother's?

8. What special gift did Harry get on his first Christmas morning at Hogwarts?

9. What animal is produced by Harry's patronus spell?

10. Who did Harry share his first kiss with?

Hermione - Part 1

11. What is Hermione's middle name?

12. What animal is Hermione's patronus?

13. Who does Hermione attend the yule ball with?

14. What device did Hermione use to fit in her extra classes?

15. What is the name of Hermione's pet cat?

16. What effect did the densaugeo spell have on Hermione?

17. In which subject did Hermione not get an outstanding grade O.W.L.?

18. What spell does Hermione use on Neville in the first book?

19. What profession are both Hermione's parents?

20. In which month is Hermione's birthday?

Ron – Part 1

21. What colour is Ron's hair?

22. What is Ron's middle name?

23. How many siblings does Ron have?

24. What does Ron get from his mum after using the flying car to get to school?

25. What did Ron buy Harry for his 13th birthday?

26. What did Ron try to repair his wand with?

27. Which character does Ron play in the game of chess in the first book?

28. True or false: Ron is pure-blood?

29. Which animal is Ron most scared of?

30. What quidditch position does Ron play?

Hogwarts - Part 1

31. What does the Hogwarts motto *Draco Dormiens Nunquam Titillandus* mean?

32. What object decides which houses the students will go into?

33. What colour is the Slytherin banner?

34. Who – or what – is Peeves?

35. What are the creatures that pull the Hogwarts carriages called?

36. What is the password to the Gryffindor common room in Harry's first year?

37. Which four animals are on the Hogwarts coat of arms?

38. In Harry's first year at Hogwarts, whose name is the first to be called out for sorting?

39. How many items are there on Filch's list of forbidden objects?

40. What is the password to open the prefects' bathroom?

The Wizarding World - Part 1

41. What are the three different forms of wizarding currency?

42. Who guards the wizarding prison of Azkaban?

43. What is the name of the wizard's hospital?

44. Who greets you at reception there?

45. And who founded it?

46. What is the name of the wizard high court of law?

47. Name the main wizarding newspaper.

48. What is the name of the all-wizard village children can visit (with permission from their parents)?

49. And what do the Harry, Ron and Hermione buy to drink there?

50. From what material is a remembrall made?

Beasts and Animals - Part 1

51.   What is Fluffy guarding in the first book?

52.   And what puts Fluffy to sleep?

53.   What is the name of Neville's toad?

54.   What is the name of the Weasley family's owl?

55.   What is the name of the hippogriff in the third book?

56.   And when he is given a new name, what is it?

57.   What sort of dog is Fang?

58.   What creature is hiding in the Chamber of Secrets?

59.   The blood of which creature kept Lord Voldemort alive in the first book?

60.   And at what age does this creature grow its horns?

Quidditch – Part 1

61. What are the three balls used in quidditch called?

62. How many points is it worth to catch the smallest ball?

63. How many players are in a quidditch team?

64. What are the playing positions in quidditch?

65. Who are Ron's favourite quidditch team?

66. What type of broomstick is Harry given in the first book?

67. Who is captain of the Gryffindor quidditch team when Harry joins Hogwarts?

68. Who was responsible for the rogue bludger in the second book?

69. Who was the captain of Slytherin's quidditch team in Harry's first year?

70. How many quidditch fouls are there?

Spells and Potions – Part 1

71. What is the name for the language used when talking to snakes?

72. What is the incantation for the levitation spell?

73. Which spell would you use to disarm an opponent?

74. How many unforgivable curses are there?

75. And can you name them?

76. Which is the worst of these, and what is it known as?

77. What spell is used to open doors?

78. Which word lights up a wand?

79. What is the spell to repel a boggart?

80. What words are used to produce a patronus charm?

Other Characters - Part 1

81. Who is the headmaster at Hogwarts in Harry's first year?

82. What are *He Who Must Not Be Named*'s supporters called?

83. Who runs The Three Broomsticks?

84. Who is the conductor on the Knight Bus?

85. And who is the driver?

86. Who was the creator of the Philosopher's Stone?

87. Who is the main commentator at Hogwarts for the quidditch matches?

88. What's the name of Colin Creevey's brother?

89. What is the name of Sirius Black's younger brother?

90. Who was killed by a forbidden curse instead of Harry?

Books and the Like - Part 1

91. What colour are howlers?

92. Rita Skeeter is a reporter for which newspaper?

93. Where did Hermione read about the ceiling at Hogwarts?

94. And who wrote it?

95. What must you do to the *Monster Book of Monsters* to open it?

96. Which magazine test rides all new broomsticks?

97. What is the name of the best-selling wizard magazine?

98. What award did *Witch Weekly* give Gilderoy Lockhart?

99. Who wrote *A History of Magic*?

100. Harry borrowed a copy of *Advanced Potion Making*; who did it belong to previously?

The Weasley Family - Part 1

101. What are Mr & Mrs Weasley's first names?

102. Which of the Weasleys is taken into the Chamber of Secrets?

103. What is the make and model of the flying car?

104. What is the name of the house where the Weasleys live?

105. How many hands does the Weasley family's clock there have?

106. Who does Ginny date before Harry?

107. What do Fred and George use to listen into conversations?

108. Which member of the Weasley family has a pony-tail and an earring?

109. And who is he engaged to?

110. In which department was Mr Weasley found after being attacked?

Hogwarts Teachers - Part 1

111. Who teaches charms?

112. Who teaches transfiguration?

113. And how long has he or she been at Hogwarts?

114. What animal can he or she turn into?

115. Who teaches history of magic?

116. What is Professor Lupin's secret?

117. What is Professor Sprout's first name?

118. Who was headmaster when Tom Riddle was at Hogwarts?

119. Who taught care of magical creatures before Hagrid?

120. What secret did Harry discover about Filch which might explain his grumpy demeanour?

General Knowledge – Part 1

121. Which plant likes to wrap itself around its victims?

122. What language do Merpeople speak?

123. To which local comprehensive school was Harry due to go?

124. How did Sirius Black escape from prison?

125. And what name do the trio refer to him as?

126. What part of you is hidden in a horcrux?

127. Which sickly-sweet (by appearance, anyway!) teacher became the new defence against the dark arts teacher in the fifth book?

128. Which family did Dobby serve?

129. What colour is the knight bus?

130. In which English county does Nicolas Flamel live?

Shops

131. Where did Harry buy his wand?

132. How many galleons does it cost?

133. Who owns the ice cream parlour in Diagon Alley?

134. What are the names of the two pubs in Hogsmeade?

135. What is the name of Fred and George's business in the later books?

136. And what is its address?

137. What does Madam Malkin sell?

138. What is the name of the main sweet shop in Hogsmeade?

139. Where would you go in Diagon Alley to buy a pet?

140. How much does it cost for a course of apparition lessons?

Dumbledore

141. What bird does Professor Dumbledore keep as a pet?

142. And what item does it bring to Harry in the Chamber of Secrets?

143. What has a cockroach cluster got to do with Dumbledore?

144. What mysterious magical items are Harry and Dumbledore trying to find in the latter books?

145. And how many does Dumbledore believe there are?

146. Where does Dumbledore store his excess memories?

147. Which wizard did Dumbledore defeat in 1945?

148. What stuffed creature was atop the witch's hat that came out of the cracker Dumbledore and Snape pulled?

149. Professor Dumbledore has a scar above his left knee in the shape of what?

150. How many uses of dragon blood did Dumbledore discover?

He Who Must Not Be Named

151. What is His name (after he changed it)?

152. What is the name of His snake?

153. True or false: He is pure-blood?

154. How many brothers did He have?

155. What is the length of His wand?

156. Who paid for Him to attend Hogwarts?

157. Who did He go to work for when he left Hogwarts?

158. How much did His mother sell a particular locket for?

159. What three things do He and Harry have in common?

160. What is the name of the village where the Riddles lived?

Hagrid

161. What did Hagrid give Harry for Christmas in the first book?

162. And what was his official job title at the time?

163. Where does Hagrid keep his wand?

164. What was the name of Hagrid's dragon?

165. And what type of dragon is he?

166. What did Hagrid give to Harry for his thirteenth birthday?

167. Who does Hagrid believe is also a half-giant?

168. Which of Hagrid's parents was a giant?

169. And what was he or she called?

170. What is the name of the giant that Hagrid brings back with him from a trip away from Hogwarts?

Harry - Part 2

171. What was the number of Harry's room at the Leaky Cauldron?

172. What interesting item did Harry find after his night visit to the library the first Christmas that he was at Hogwarts?

173. Who did Harry meet in the Leaky Cauldron before the start of his first year at Hogwarts?

174. Who looked after Harry when the Dursleys went out?

175. What was Harry's mother's maiden name?

176. What creature's feathers do Harry and Lord Voldemort have as part of their wands?

177. What does the scar on the back of Harry's hand say?

178. Which wood is Harry's wand made of?

179. Which wood was his father's wand made from?

180. Which career does Harry want to have?

Hermione - Part 2

181. What does S.P.E.W. stand for?

182. And how much does it cost to join?

183. What did Hermione knit in relation to this?

184. On the subject of abbreviations, what does DA stand for?

185. And what does Hermione give to every member?

186. What spell did Hermione cast on a student during the quidditch trials?

187. And on whom did she cast it?

188. Whose party did she then take him to?

189. What exam clashes with Hermione's ancient runes one?

190. Who is Hermione married to at the end of the final book?

Ron - Part 2

191. Who does Ron ask for an autograph in the fourth book?

192. When Ron gets a new wand in the third book, what is it made of?

193. And how long was it?

194. Who gave Pigwidgeon to Ron following the loss of Scabbers?

195. And who actually named it?

196. What does Dumbledore bequeath Ron in his will?

197. What did Harry buy Ron for his 17th birthday?

198. What did Ron eat that contained a love potion?

199. On the subject of girls, who did Ron date, kiss and break up with?

200. When Ron was poisoned what did Harry use to save him?

Hogwarts - Part 2

201. Who haunts the girls' toilets on the first floor?

202. How many secret passages lead from Hogwarts to Hogsmeade?

203. Who usually guards the entrance to the Gryffindor Tower?

204. What are O.W.L.s?

205. What is the place that the DA practice in called?

206. How many schools take part in the Triwizard Tournament?

207. Name them!

208. And what is now the minimum age for a competitor?

209. What does the flying car crash into at Hogwarts?

210. What was Quirrell trying to get out of the mirror in the first book?

Beasts and Animals – Part 2

211. What got into the castle on Hallowe'en night of Harry's first term?

212. What type of owl is Hedwig?

213. What kind of creature is Aragog?

214. And who attended his funeral?

215. What did Professor Slughorn want from Aragog's body?

216. Where is Kreacher sent to work?

217. Name the centaur who helped Harry in the forbidden forest.

218. Which animal represents 'The Grim'?

219. What is Sirius's house-elf called?

220. On what does Professor Moody demonstrate the Imperius Curse?

Quidditch - Part 2

221. Who was the only girl on the Ravenclaw quidditch team?

222. Who insists that Harry and his friends support the Ireland quidditch team at the world cup?

223. And who did Ireland beat in the semi-final?

224. Who did they play in the final?

225. And which of these two won?

226. Who refereed the final?

227. How much were a pair of omniculars at the world cup?

228. Which type of wood is the handle of a Nimbus 2000 made from?

229. Who banned Harry from playing quidditch in his fifth year?

230. What make of broom does Harry get in his third year?

Spells and Potions - Part 2

231. Which spell reveals the last spell a wand performed?

232. Harry, Ron and Hermione make which special potion in the second book to fool Malfoy?

233. What is mandrake root used for?

234. Which potion does Professor Lupin take regularly?

235. What is felix felicis?

236. And how long does it take to prepare?

237. Which plant did Harry use during one of the Triwizard challenges?

238. What happens when someone takes the potion veritaserum?

239. The pus from which plant is a powerful cure for acne?

240. And what does that plant look like?

Other Characters – Part 2

241. Which animal can Rita Skeeter turn into?

242. What is Fleur Delacour's sister called?

243. Who does Tonks fall in love with?

244. Who edits *The Quibbler*?

245. Who is the landlord of the Leaky Cauldron?

246. What does Nearly Headless Nick celebrate each year to which Harry and his friends are once invited?

247. Into which Hogwarts house was Owen Cauldwell sorted?

248. What are the first names of Sirius's evil cousins?

249. Who replaced Cornelius Fudge as Minister of Magic?

250. Who accidentally opens a parcel with a cursed necklace in it?

The Weasley Family – Part 2

251. What magical item do the Weasley twins give to Harry in his third year?

252. What is Mr Weasley's nickname for his wife?

253. How many galleons was Mr Weasley fined for bewitching a car?

254. What does Mrs Weasley give Harry for supper when he arrives at the Burrow before starting his sixth year at Hogwarts?

255. Who is Percy Weasley's boss?

256. And what does he call Percy?

257. How many O.W.L.s did Percy take?

258. What is the name of Percy's (actual) owl?

259. What department is Mr Weasley the head of?

260. How many galleons were in the Weasleys' vault at Gringotts?

The Dursleys

261. What is the name of Uncle Vernon's company?

262. How many presents did Dudley get for his birthday in the first book?

263. What do Dudley's gang call him?

264. And what does Aunt Petunia call him?

265. What school do the Dursleys say Harry goes to?

266. How many dogs does Aunt Marge have in total?

267. And which department was sent to deflate her?

268. What colour were the tailcoats worn at Smeltings School?

269. Which one of the Dursleys throws ornaments at Mr Weasley?

270. To which hotel did Uncle Vernon take his family and Harry to escape Harry's initial letters from Hogwarts?

Harry - Part 3

271. Who tied Harry to a gravestone?

272. What extra subject did Harry take with Snape?

273. From which wood was Harry's mother's wand made from?

274. Which three major items did Harry inherit from Sirius?

275. Who did Harry take to Slughorn's party?

276. Which street does Harry end up in the first time he travels by floo powder?

277. Who did Harry duel with at the "duelling club"?

278. Which ghost did Harry meet when he was in the lake?

279. What was the name of the road on which Harry first saw the knight bus?

280. And when he gets on, what name does Harry give Stan instead of his own?

Hogwarts Teachers - Part 2

281. What is Professor Flitwick's first name?

282. What role does Professor Tofty have?

283. Which potions teacher returns to Hogwarts after a long absence?

284. Professor Grubby-Plank took over from which teacher?

285. Who is the new divination professor in Harry's final years?

286. What is Madame Pomfrey's first name?

287. Which dashing wizard becomes the defence against the dark arts teacher in Harry's second year?

288. Who is the head of Hufflepuff House?

289. Professor Sinistra teaches in which department at Hogwarts?

290. Who brought Colin Creevey to Madam Pomfrey?

General Knowledge - Part 2

291. What are N.E.W.T.s?

292. To where does the tunnel under the whomping willow lead?

293. Professor Trelawney's prophecy could apply to who else?

294. Who are Moony, Wormtail, Padfoot and Prongs better known as (make sure you get the correct order)?

295. Which member of the Order of the Phoenix is working for the muggle prime minister?

296. Who comes to Harry's rescue when he's hiding from Professor Lupin (in werewolf form)?

297. Which competitor wants to return to England to improve her language skills?

298. From which vault did Hagrid take something from at Gringotts?

299. What is the Gryffindor ghost's full name.

300. And how many times was he hit in the neck with a blunt axe?

Books and the Like - Part 2

301. Which book does Dumbledore bequeath to Hermione?

302. How many galleons formed the prize money in the *Daily Prophet's* 'prize galleon draw'?

303. What did Harry use to keep the *Monster Book of Monsters* shut?

304. What name got inscribed on Ron's *Advanced Potion Making* Book?

305. Who is the book's author?

306. Who wants to write Harry Potter's biography?

307. How did people who had read *Sonnets of a Sorcerer* speak for the rest of their lives?

308. In which book can you read about curse scars?

309. Who wrote *Curses and Counter Curses*?

310. Who wrote *The Dream Oracle*?

The Wizarding World – Part 2

311. How old are witches and wizards when they come of age?

312. What are the four different types of blood purity?

313. What is the main lift at the Ministry of Magic disguised as?

314. What are dark wizard catchers called?

315. What is the name of the place in London where witches and wizards go to shop?

316. Which object is used to transport wizards from one place to another at an arranged time?

317. How long ago was the Triwizard Tournament started?

318. How many people have survived the Avada Kedavra curse?

319. What is the address of Sirius's house?

320. What is the name of the department store which hides the main wizarding hospital?

Professor Snape

321. What job are we told that Snape really wants?

322. Where did Professor Snape meet with Quirrell so they wouldn't be overheard?

323. What was James Potter's nickname for Snape?

324. Name the potion that Professor Snape threatens to use on Harry?

325. Where does Professor Snape live?

326. What did Mrs Malfoy want Snape to make?

327. What is the name of Snape's mother?

328. And his father?

329. Who went to visit Snape in his home?

330. Who does Snape make a monthly potion for whilst he is at Hogwarts?

Beasts and Animals – Part 3

331. What kind of creature is Ronan?

332. Which werewolf bit Remus Lupin?

333. The sound of which creature can kill a Basilisk?

334. Which two types of dragon are found in the British Isles?

335. What animal's blood should you feed (with brandy) to a dragon?

336. Which creatures guard the lake in the cave where Harry finds a horcrux with Dumbledore?

337. What is the name of Aunt Marge's dog?

338. How many giants does Hagrid think there are left?

339. And who is the Gurg?

340. What is the name of Hepzibah Smith's house elf?

Quidditch - Part 3

341. Who was the last Gryffindor seeker to help win the quidditch cup?

342. What position did Lockhart say he played at quidditch?

343. How many seconds does it take a Firebolt to accelerate from zero to 150 miles per hour?

344. What quidditch team does Cho Chang support?

345. Who does Oliver Wood play for after leaving Hogwarts?

346. So who takes over from him at Gryffindor?

347. Who captains the Holyhead Harpies?

348. How many years had it been since Britain last hosted the quidditch World Cup?

349. What colour was the dark mark skull in the sky when Britain did host it after all that time?

350. And which house elf did Harry meet there?

Other Characters – Part 3

351. Who were Sirius Black's parents?

352. Who is linked to both Hogwarts staff and the hospital?

353. What did Apollyon Pringle do at Hogwarts when Mrs Weasley was a student there?

354. Who were the first two death eaters to make it to the top of the astronomy tower after Draco?

355. Who liked being burned at the stake so much she allowed it to happen forty-seven times?

356. Who does Harry ask the minister to release from prison?

357. What is Neville's great uncle called?

358. What is Mrs Figg's first name?

359. Whose father was an auror called Frank?

360. Who is Sirius's great-great-grandfather?

Draco Malfoy and Friends

361. What did Malfoy take that belonged to Neville in book 1?

362. What are the first names of Crabbe and Goyle?

363. What offensive term did Malfoy first call Hermione in their second year?

364. Which shop does Draco attend in Knockturn Alley?

365. Who does Harry ask to watch Malfoy together?

366. How are Crabbe and Goyle disguised when on look out?

367. Who did Draco take to the yule ball?

368. To what size did Draco's nose swell during one of Professor Snape's potions classes?

369. Who dressed up as dementors to scare Harry, along with Malfoy, Crabbe and Goyle?

370. Which spell did Professor Snape suggest Draco cast on Harry at the duelling club?

The Weasley Family – Part 3

371. What does Ron vomit after casting a spell with his broken wand?

372. And what bit of 'specialist equipment' is given to him to help recover?

373. What are George and Fred's fireworks called?

374. What present did Fred and George try to send to Harry when he was in the hospital wing?

375. What did Bill develop a liking for after being bitten by a werewolf?

376. Which Ministry department does Percy Weasley first work for?

377. What is the name of Percy's girlfriend?

378. Who accompanies Percy to the Weasley's house on Christmas Day?

379. Who provided the twins with venomous tentacula seeds?

380. Who is Mrs Weasley's favourite singer?

Spells and Potions - Part 3

381. What potion would Madam Pomfrey use to help cure colds?

382. What is it called when you leave half of yourself behind when apparating?

383. What potion do Asphodel & Wormwood make?

384. What is the spell to conjure the dark mark?

385. What simple spell would you use to start a fire?

386. What spell does Harry use to dangle Ron by his ankles?

387. What are the three things to think of when casting the apparition spell?

388. What spell is used to put out the fire at Hagrid's?

389. What ancient language do many spells rely on?

390. Which spell would you use to damage an opponent's eyesight?

General Knowledge - Part 3

391. Where is the nearest portkey to the Weasleys' home?

392. Who is appointed as Buckbeak's executioner?

393. How much did the Dursleys once give to Harry for his Christmas present?

394. How many Valentine's Day cards did Gilderoy Lockhart say he had received?

395. What length of parchment did Professor Binns ask for on the medieval assembly of European wizards?

396. Which member of the order is a metamorphmagus?

397. Who was caught smuggling flying carpets into Britain?

398. When did The Gryffindor Ghost die?

399. How many people could travel on Barty Crouch's Grandfather's Magic Carpet?

400. What are the four types of dragon used in the Triwizard Tournament?

The Answers

Harry - Part 1

1. 31st July

2. 4 Privet Drive, Little Whinging

3. Hagrid

4. A Lightning Bolt

5. A Boa-Constrictor

6. James

7. Lily

8. An Invisibility Cloak

9. A Stag

10. Cho Chan

Hermione - Part 1

Ron - Part 1

21. Ginger

22. Bilius

23. Six

24. A Howler

25. A Pocket Sneakoscope

26. Spellotape

27. A Knight

28. True

29. A Spider

30. Keeper

Hogwarts – Part 1

The Wizarding World - Part 1

Beasts and Animals - Part 1

51.   The Philosophers Stone

52.   Music (specifically a Harp)

53.   Trevor

54.   Errol

55.   Buckbeak

56.   Witherwings

57.   A Boarhound

58.   Basilisk

59.   The Unicorn

60.   4

Quidditch - Part 1

61. Bludger, Quaffle and Golden Snitch

62. 150

63. 7

64. Beater, Chaser, Keeper and Seeker

65. Chudley Cannons

66. A Nimbus 2000

67. Oliver Wood

68. Dobby

69. Marcus Flint

70. 700

Spells and Potions - Part 1

Other Characters - Part 1

Books and the Like - Part 1

91. Red

92. The Daily Prophet

93. Hogwarts: A History

94. Chroniclus Punnet

95. Stroke its Spine

96. Which Broomstick

97. The Quibbler

98. Most Charming Smile

99. Bathilda Bagshot

100. The Half Blood Prince

The Weasley Family - Part 1

Hogwarts Teachers - Part 1

111. Professor Flitwick

112. Professor McGonagall

113. 39 years

114. A Tabby Cat

115. Professor Binns

116. He is a Werewolf

117. Pomona

118. Professor Dippet

119. Professor Kettleburn

120. He is a Squib

General Knowledge – Part 1

121. Devil's Snare

122. Mermish

123. Stonewall High

124. He transformed into a Dog

125. Snuffles

126. Your Soul

127. Professor Umbridge

128. The Malfoys

129. Purple

130. Devon

Shops

Dumbledore

141. A Phoenix

142. The Sorting Hat and Godric Gryffindor's Sword

143. It was the password to his office

144. Horcruxes

145. Six

146. In a Pensieve

147. Grindelwald

148. A Vulture

149. A Map of the London Underground

150. Twelve

He Who Must Not Be Named

151. Lord Voldemort

152. Nagini

153. False

154. None

155. Thirteen and a half inches

156. The Hogwarts assistance fund

157. Borgin and Burke's

158. Ten Galleons

159. They are both Half-Bloods, they are both Orphans, and they both speak Parseltongue.

160. Little Hangleton

Hagrid

Harry - Part 2

Hermione - Part 2

181. (The) Society for the Promotion of Elfish Welfare

182. Two Sickles

183. Hats and Socks for the House Elves

184. Dumbledore's Army

185. A Fake Galleon

186. Confundus

187. Cormac McLaggen

188. Professor Slughorn's

189. Charms

190. Ron

Ron - Part 2

191. Viktor Krum

192. Willow with a Unicorn Tail Hair Core

193. Fourteen Inches

194. Sirius Black

195. Ginny

196. The Deluminator

197. Quidditch Keeper's Gloves

198. A Chocolate Cauldron

199. Lavender Brown

200. Bezoar

Hogwarts - Part 2

Beasts and Animals - Part 2

Quidditch - Part 2

221. Cho Chang

222. Seamus Finnegan

223. Peru

224. Bulgaria

225. Ireland

226. Hassan Mostafa

227. 10 Galleons

228. Mahogany

229. Professor Umbridge

230. A Firebolt

Spells and Potions – Part 2

Other Characters - Part 2

The Weasley Family – Part 2

251. The Marauder's Map

252. Mollywobbles

253. Fifty

254. Onion Soup

255. Barty Crouch

256. Weatherby

257. Twelve

258. Hermes

259. The Misuse of Muggle Artefacts Office

260. One

The Dursleys

Harry - Part 3

Hogwarts Teachers - Part 2

General Knowledge – Part 2

291. Nastily Exhausting Wizarding Tests

292. The Shrieking Shack

293. Neville Longbottom

294. Remus Lupin, Peter Pettigrew, Sirius Black and James Potter

295. Kingsley Shacklebolt

296. Buckbeak

297. Fleur Delacour

298. 713

299. Sir Nicholas de Mimsy-Porpington

300. Forty-five

Books and the Like – Part 2

301. The Tales of Beedle the Bard

302. Seven Hundred

303. A Belt

304. Roonil Wazlib

305. Libatius Borage

306. Eldred Worple

307. In Limericks

308. Common Magical Ailments and Afflictions

309. Vindictus Viridian

310. Inigo Imago

The Wizarding World - Part 2

Professor Snape

Beasts and Animals – Part 3

Quidditch - Part 3

Other Characters - Part 3

Draco Malfoy and Friends

The Weasley Family - Part 3

371. Slugs

372. A Bucket

373. Weasleys' Wildfire Whiz-Bangs

374. A Toilet Seat

375. Rare Steak

376. The Department of International Magical Co-operation

377. Penelope Clearwater

378. Rufus Scrimgeour

379. Mundungus Fletcher

380. Celestina Warbeck

Spells and Potions – Part 3

General Knowledge - Part 3

391. Stoatshead Hill

392. Walden MacNair

393. Fifty Pence

394. Forty-six

395. Three Feet

396. Nymphadora Tonks

397. Ali Bashir

398. The 31st October 1492

399. Twelve

400. The Chinese Fireball, The Hungarian Horntail, The Swedish Short-Snout and The Welsh Green

Also by Jack Goldstein

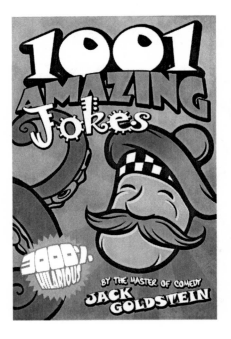

Do you want a joke for every situation? Are you sure you're prepared for the moment when your audience's heads fall off and their sides split? Master of comedy Jack Goldstein is proud to present this collection of 1001 of the funniest jokes in the history of the world. There's a food joke that pasta be the best you've ever read, and the ones about space are out of this world. The animal jokes will have you roaring in delight, but be careful - doctor, doctor might not have a laughter cure. Organised into categories so you can find the joke you want quickly, this is the perfect addition for any budding comedian's bookshelf.

CPSIA information can be obtained at www.ICGtesting.com
Printed in the USA
LVOW08s2231041215

465236LV00001B/1/P